PLEDGED
to the Dead

PLEDGED
to the Dead
SEABURY QUINN

ÆGYPAN PRESS

From *Weird Tales,* October, 1937.

Special thanks to Sankar Viswanathan, Greg Weeks, and the
Online Distributed Proofreading Team (which can be found
at http://www.pgdp.net).

Pledged to the Dead
A publication of
ÆGYPAN PRESS

www.aegypan.com

A tale of a lover who was pledged to a sweetheart who had been in her grave for more than a century, and of the striking death that menaced him — a story of Jules de Grandin.

*T*he autumn dusk had stained the sky with shadows and orange oblongs traced the windows in my neighbors' homes as Jules de Grandin and I sat sipping kaiserschmarrn and coffee in the study after dinner. *"Mon Dieu,"* the little Frenchman sighed, "I have the *mal du pays,* my friend. The little children run and play along the roadways at Saint Cloud, and on the Île de France the pastry cooks set up their booths. *Corbleu,* it takes the strength of character not to stop and buy those cakes of so much taste and fancy! The Napoléons, they are crisp and fragile as a coquette's promise, the éclairs filled with cool, sweet cream, the cream-puffs all aglow with cherries. Just to see them is to love life better. They —"

The shrilling of the door-bell startled me. The pressure on the button must have been that of one who leant against it. "Doctor Trowbridge; I must see him right away!" a woman's voice demanded as Nora McGinnis, my household factotum, grudgingly responded to the hail.

"Th' docthor's offiss hours is over, ma'am," Nora answered frigidly. "Ha'f past nine ter eleven in th' marnin', an' two ter four in th' afthernoon is when he sees his patients. If it's an urgent case ye have there's lots o' good young docthors in th' neighborhood, but Docthor Trowbridge —"

"Is he here?" the visitor demanded sharply.

"He is, an' he's afther digestin' his dinner — an' an illigant dinner it wuz, though I do say so as shouldn't — an' he can't be disturbed —"

"He'll see me, all right. Tell him it's Nella Bentley, and I've *got* to talk to him!"

De Grandin raised an eyebrow eloquently. "The fish at the aquarium have greater privacy than we, my friend," he murmured, but broke off as the visitor came clacking down the hall on high French heels and rushed into the study half a dozen paces in advance of my thoroughly disapproving and more than semi-scandalized Nora.

"Doctor Trowbridge, won't you help me?" cried the girl as she fairly leaped across the study and flung her arms about my shoulders. "I can't tell Dad or Mother, they wouldn't understand; so you're the only one — oh, excuse me, I thought you were alone!" Her face went crimson as she saw de Grandin standing by the fire.

"It's quite all right, my dear," I soothed, freeing myself from her almost hysterical clutch. "This is Doctor de Grandin, with whom I've been associated many times; I'd be glad to have the benefit of his advice, if you don't mind."

She gave him her hand and a wan smile as I performed the introduction, but her eyes warmed quickly as he raised her fingers to his lips with a soft *"Enchanté, Mademoiselle."* Women, animals and children took instinctively to Jules de Grandin.

Nella dropped her coat of silky shaven lamb and sank down on the study couch, her slim young figure molded in her knitted dress of coral rayon as revealingly as though she had been cased in plastic cellulose. She has long, violet eyes and a long mouth; smooth, dark hair parted in the middle; a small straight nose, and a small pointed chin. Every line of her is long, but definitely feminine; breasts and hips and throat and legs all delicately curved, without a hint of angularity.

"I've come to see you about Ned," she volunteered as de Grandin lit her cigarette and she sent a nervous smoke-stream gushing from between red, trembling lips. "He − he's trying to run out on me!"

"You mean Ned Minton?" I asked, wondering what a middle-aged physician could prescribe for wandering Romeos.

"I certainly do mean Ned Minton," she replied, "and I mean business, too. The darn, romantic fool!"

De Grandin's slender brows arched upward till they nearly met the beige-blond hair that slanted sleekly backward from his forehead. *"Pardonnez-moi,"* he murmured. "Did I understand correctly, *Mademoiselle?* Your *amoureux* − how do you say him? − sweetheart? − has shown a disposition toward unfaithfulness, yet you accuse him of romanticism?"

"He's not unfaithful, that's the worst of it. He's faithful as Tristan and the chevalier Bayard lumped together, *sans peur et sans reproche*, you know. Says we can't get married, 'cause −"

"Just a moment, dear," I interrupted as I felt my indignation mounting. "D'ye mean the miserable young puppy cheated, and now wants to welch −"

*H*er blue eyes widened, then the little laughter-wrinkles formed around them. "You dear old mid-Victorian!" she broke in. "No, he ain't done wrong by our

Nell, and I'm not asking you to take your shotgun down and force him to make me an honest woman. Suppose we start at the beginning: then we'll get things straight.

"You assisted at both our débuts, I've been told; you've known Ned and me since we were a second old apiece, haven't you?"

I nodded.

"Know we've always been crazy about each other, too; in grammar school, high school and college, don't you?"

"Yes," I agreed.

"All right. We've been engaged ever since our freshman year at Beaver. Ned just had his frat pin long enough to pin it on my shoulder-strap at the first freshman dance. Everything was set for us to stand up in the chancel and say 'I do' this June; then Ned's company sent him to New Orleans last December." She paused, drew deeply at her cigarette, crushed its fire out in an ash-tray, and set a fresh one glowing.

"That started it. While he was down there it seemed that he got playful. Mixed up with some glamourous Creole gal." Once more she lapsed into silence and I could see the heartbreak showing through the armor of her flippant manner.

"You mean he fell in love —"

"I certainly do *not!* If he had, I'd have handed back his ring and said 'Bless you, me children', even if I had to bite my heart in two to do it; but this is no case of a new love crowding out the old. Ned still loves me; never stopped loving me. That's what makes it all seem crazy as a hashish-eater's dream. He was on the loose in New Orleans, doing the town with a crowd of local boys, and prob'ly had too many Ramos fizzes. Then he barged into this Creole dame's place, and —" she broke off with a gallant effort at a smile. "I guess young fellows aren't so different nowadays than they were when you were growing up, sir. Only today we don't believe in sprinkling perfume in the family cesspool. Ned cheated, that's the bald truth of it; he didn't stop loving me, and he hasn't stopped now, but I wasn't there and that other girl was, and there were no conventions to be recognized. Now he's fairly melting with remorse, says he's not worthy of me — wants to break off our engagement, while he spends a lifetime doing penance for a moment's folly."

"But good heavens," I expostulated, "if you're willing to forgive —"

"You're telling me!" she answered bitterly. "We've been over it a hundred times. This isn't 1892; even nice girls know the facts of life today, and while I'm no more anxious than the next one to put through a deal in shopworn goods, I still love Ned, and I don't intend to let a single indiscretion rob us of our happiness. I —" the hard exterior veneer of modernism melted from her like an autumn ice-glaze melting in the warm October sun, and the tears coursed down her cheeks, cutting little valleys in her carefully-applied make-up. "He's my man, Doctor," she sobbed bitterly. "I've loved him since we made mud-pies together; I'm hungry, thirsty for him. He's everything to me, and if he follows out this fool renunciation he seems set on, it'll kill me!"

De Grandin tweaked a waxed mustache-end thoughtfully. "You exemplify the practicality of woman, *Mademoiselle*; I applaud your sound, hard common sense," he told her. "Bring this silly young romantic foolish one to me. I will tell him —"

"But he won't come," I interrupted. "I know these hard-minded young asses. When a lad is set on being stubborn —"

"Will you go to work on him if I can get him here?" interjected Nella.

"Of a certitude, *Mademoiselle.*"

"You won't think me forward or unmaidenly?"

"This is a medical consultation, *Mademoiselle.*"

"All right; be in the office this time tomorrow night. I'll have my wandering boy friend here if I have to bring him in an ambulance."

*H*er performance matched her promise almost too closely for our comfort. We had just finished dinner next night when the frenzied shriek of tortured brakes, followed by a crash and the tinkling spatter of smashed glass, sounded in the street before the house, and in a moment feet dragged heavily across the porch. We were at the door before the bell could buzz, and in the disk of brightness sent down by the porch light saw Nella bent half double, stumbling forward with a man's arm draped across her shoulders. His feet scuffed blindly on the boards, as though they had forgot the trick of walking, or as if all strength had left his knees. His head hung forward, lolling drunkenly; a spate of blood ran down his face and smeared his collar.

"Good Lord!" I gasped. "What —"

"Get him in the surgery — quick!" the girl commanded in a whisper. "I'm afraid I rather overdid it."

Examination showed the cut across Ned's forehead was more bloody than extensive, while the scalp-wound which plowed backward from his hairline needed but a few quick stitches.

Nella whispered to us as we worked. "I got him to go riding with me in my runabout. Just as we got here I let out a scream and swung the wheel hard over to the right. I was braced for it, but Ned was unprepared, and went right through the windshield when I ran the car into the curb. Lord, I thought I'd killed him when I saw the blood — you do think he'll come through all right, don't you, Doctor?"

"No thanks to you if he does, you little ninny!" I retorted angrily. "You might have cut his jugular with your confounded foolishness. If —"

"*S-s-sh,* he's coming out of it!" she warned. "Start talking to him like a Dutch uncle; I'll be waiting in the study if you want me," and with a tattoo of high heels she left us with our patient.

"Nella! Is she all right?" Ned cried as he half roused from the surgery table. "We had an accident —"

"But certainly, *Monsieur,*" de Grandin soothed. "You were driving past our house when a child ran out before your car and *Mademoiselle* was forced to swerve aside to keep from hitting it. You were cut about the face, but she escaped all injury. Here" — he raised a glass of brandy to the patient's lips — "drink this. Ah, so. That is better, *n'est-ce-pas?*"

For a moment he regarded Ned in silence, then, abruptly: "You are distrait, *Monsieur.* When we brought you in we were forced to give you a small whiff of ether while we patched your cuts, and in your delirium you said —"

The color which had come into Ned's cheeks as the fiery cognac warmed his veins drained out again, leaving him as ghastly as a corpse. "Did Nella hear me?" he asked hoarsely. "Did I blab —"

"Compose yourself, *Monsieur,*" de Grandin bade. "She heard nothing, but it would be well if we heard more. I think I understand your difficulty. I am a physician and a Frenchman and no prude. This renunciation which you make is but the noble gesture. You have been unfortunate, and now you fear. Have courage; no infection is so bad there is no remedy —"

Ned's laugh was hard and brittle as the tinkle of a breaking glass. "I only wish it were the thing you think," he interrupted. "I'd have you give me salvarsan and see what happened; but there isn't any treatment I can take for this. I'm not delirious, and I'm not crazy, gentlemen; I know just what I'm saying. Insane as it may sound, I'm pledged to the dead, and there isn't any way to bail me out."

"*Eh*, what is it you say?" de Grandin's small blue eyes were gleaming with the light of battle as he caught the occult implication in Ned's declaration. "Pledged to the dead? *Comment cela?*"

*N*ed raised himself unsteadily and balanced on the table edge.

"It happened in New Orleans last winter," he answered. "I'd finished up my business and was on the loose, and thought I'd walk alone through the *Vieux Carré* — the old French Quarter. I'd had dinner at Antoine's and stopped around at the Old Absinthe House for a few drinks, then strolled down to the French Market for a cup of chicory coffee and some doughnuts. Finally I walked down Royal Street to look at Madame Lalaurie's old mansion; that's the famous haunted house, you know. I wanted to see if I could find a ghost. Good Lord, I *wanted* to!

"The moon was full that night, but the house was still as old Saint Denis Cemetery, so after peering through the iron grilles that shut the courtyard from the street for half an hour or so, I started back toward Canal Street.

"I'd almost reached Bienville Street when just as I passed one of those funny two-storied iron-grilled balconies so many of the old houses have I heard something drop on the sidewalk at my feet. It was a japonica, one of those roselike flowers they grow in the courtyard gardens down there. When I looked up, a girl was laughing at me from the second story of the balcony. *'Mon fleuron, monsieur, s'il vous plait,'* she called, stretching down a white arm for the bloom.

"The moonlight hung about her like a veil of silver tissue, and I could see her plainly as though it had been noon. Most New Orleans girls are dark. She was fair, her hair was very fine and silky and about the color of a frosted chestnut-burr. She wore it in a long bob with curls around her face and neck, and I knew without being told that those ringlets weren't put in with a hot iron. Her face was pale, colorless and fine-textured as a magnolia petal, but her lips were brilliant crimson. There was something reminiscent of those ladies you see pictured in Directoire prints about her; small, regular features, straight, white, high-waisted gown tied with a wide girdle underneath her bosom, low, round-cut neck and tiny, ball-puff sleeves that left her lovely arms uncovered to the shoulder. She was like Rose Beauharnais or Madame de Fontenay, except for her fair hair, and her eyes. Her eyes were like an Eastern slave's, languishing and passionate, even when she laughed. And she was laughing then, with a throaty, almost caressing laugh as I tossed the flower up to her and she leant across the iron railing, snatching at it futilely as it fell just short of reach.

"*'C'est sans profit,'* she laughed at last. 'Your skill is too small or my arm too short, *m'sieur*. Bring it up to me.'

"'You mean for me to come up there?' I asked.

"'But certainly. I have teeth, but will not bite you — maybe.'

"The street door to the house was open; I pushed it back, groped my way along a narrow hall and climbed a flight of winding stairs. She was waiting for me on the balcony, lovelier, close up, if that were possible, than when I'd seen her from the sidewalk. Her gown was China silk, so sheer and clinging that the shadow of her charming figure showed against its rippling folds like a lovely silhouette; the sash which bound it was a six-foot length of rainbow ribbon tied coquettishly beneath her shoulders and trailing in fringed ends almost to her dress-hem at the back; her feet were stockingless and shod with sandals fastened with cross-straps of purple grosgrain laced about the ankles. Save for the small gold rings that scintillated in her ears, she wore no ornaments of any kind.

"'*Mon fleur, m'sieur,*' she ordered haughtily, stretching out her hand; then her eyes lighted with sudden laughter and she turned her back to me, bending her head forward. 'But no, it fell into your hands; it is that you must put in its place again,' she ordered, pointing to a curl where she wished the flower set. 'Come, *m'sieur,* I wait upon you.'

"On the settee by the wall a guitar lay. She picked it up and ran her slim, pale fingers twice across the strings, sounding a soft, melancholy chord. When she began to sing, her words were slurred and languorous, and I had trouble understanding them; for the song was ancient when Bienville turned the first spadeful of earth that marked the ramparts of New Orleans:

O knights of gay Toulouse
  And sweet Beaucaire,
 Greet me my own true love
  And speak him fair. . . .

"Her voice had the throaty, velvety quality one hears in people of the Southern countries, and the words of the song seemed fairly to yearn with the sadness and passionate longing of the love-bereft. But she smiled as she put by her instrument, a curious smile, which heightened the mystery of her face, and her wide eyes seemed suddenly half questing, half drowsy, as she asked, 'Would you ride off upon your grim, pale horse and leave poor little Julie d'Ayen famishing for love, m'sieur?'

"'Ride off from you?' I answered gallantly. 'How can you ask?' A verse from Burns came to me:

Then fare thee well, my bonny lass,
And fare thee well awhile,
And I will come to thee again
An it were ten thousand mile.

"There was something avid in the look she gave me. Something more than mere gratified vanity shone in her eyes as she turned her face up to me in the moonlight. 'You mean it?' she demanded in a quivering, breathless voice.

"'Of course,' I bantered. 'How could you doubt it?'

"'Then swear it — seal the oath with blood!'

"Her eyes were almost closed, and her lips were lightly parted as she leant toward me. I could see the thin, white line of tiny, gleaming teeth behind the lush red of her lips; the tip of a pink tongue swept across her mouth, leaving it warmer, moister, redder than before; in her throat a small pulse throbbed palpitatingly. Her lips were smooth and soft as the flower-petals in her hair, but as they crushed on mine they seemed to creep about them as though endowed with a volition of their own. I could feel them gliding almost stealthily, searching greedily, it seemed, until they covered my entire mouth. Then came a sudden searing burn of pain which passed as quickly as it flashed across my lips, and she seemed inhaling deeply, desperately, as though to pump the last faint gasp of breath up from my lungs. A humming sounded in my ears; everything went dark around me as if I had been plunged in some abysmal flood; a spell of dreamy lassitude was stealing over me when she pushed me from her so abruptly that I staggered back against the iron railing of the gallery.

"*I* gasped and fought for breath like a winded swimmer coming from the water, but the half-recaptured breath seemed suddenly to catch itself unbidden in my throat, and a tingling chill went rippling up my spine. The girl had dropped down to her knees, staring at the door which let into the house, and as I looked I saw a shadow writhe across the little pool of moonlight which lay upon the sill. Three feet or so in length it was, thick through as a man's wrist, the faint light shining dully on its scaly armor and disclosing the forked lightning of its darting tongue. It was a cottonmouth — a water moccasin — deadly as a rattlesnake, but more danger-ous, for it sounds no warning before striking, and can strike when only half coiled. How it came there on the second-story gallery of a house so far from any swamp-land I had no means of knowing, but there it lay, bent in the design of a double S, its wedge-shaped head swaying on up-reared neck a scant six inches from the girl's soft bosom, its forked tongue darting deathly menace. Half paralyzed with fear and loathing, I stood there in a perfect ecstasy of horror, not daring to move hand or foot lest I aggravate the reptile into striking. But my terror changed to stark amazement as my senses slowly registered the scene. The girl was talking to the snake and — it listened as a person might have done!

"'*Non, non, grand'tante; halte là!*' she whispered. '*Cela est à moi – il est dévoué!*'

"The serpent seemed to pause uncertainly, grudgingly, as though but half convinced, then shook its head from side to side, much as an aged person might when only half persuaded by a youngster's argument. Finally, silently as a shadow, it slithered back again into the darkness of the house.

"Julie bounded to her feet and put her hands upon my shoulders.

"'You mus' go, my friend,' she whispered fiercely. 'Quickly, ere she comes again. It was not easy to convince her; she is old and very doubting. O, I am afraid – afraid!'

"She hid her face against my arm, and I could feel the throbbing of her heart against me. Her hands stole upward to my cheeks and pressed them between palms as cold as graveyard clay as she whispered, 'Look at me, *mon beau.*' Her eyes were closed, her lips were slightly parted, and beneath the arc of her long lashes I could see the glimmer of fast-forming tears. '*Embrasse moi*', she commanded in a trembling breath. 'Kiss me and go quickly, but *O mon chèr*, do not forget poor little foolish Julie d'Ayen who has put her trust in you. Come to me again tomorrow night!'

"I was reeling as from vertigo as I walked back to the Greenwald, and the bartender looked at me suspiciously when I ordered a sazarac. They've a strict rule against serving drunken men at that hotel. The liquor stung my lips like liquid flame, and I put the cocktail down half finished. When I set the fan to going and switched the light on in my room I looked into the mirror and saw two little beads of fresh, bright blood upon my lips. 'Good Lord!' I murmured stupidly as I brushed the blood away; 'she bit me!'

"It all seemed so incredible that if I had not seen the blood upon my mouth I'd have thought I suffered from some lunatic hallucination, or one too many frappés at the Absinthe House. Julie was as quaint and out of time as a Directoire print, even in a city where time stands still as it does in old New Orleans. Her costume, her half-shy boldness, her — this was simply madness, nothing less! — her conversation with that snake!

"What was it she had said? My French was none too good, and in the circumstances it was hardly possible to pay attention to her words, but if I'd understood her, she'd declared, 'He's mine; he has dedicated himself to me!' And she'd addressed that crawling horror as *'grand'tante* — great-aunt!'

"'Feller, you're as crazy as a cockroach!' I admonished my reflection in the mirror. 'But I know what'll cure you. You're taking the first train north tomorrow morning, and if I ever catch you in the *Vieux Carré* again, I'll —'

"A sibilating hiss, no louder than the noise made by steam escaping from a kettle-spout, sounded close beside my foot. There on the rug, coiled in readiness to strike, was a three-foot cottonmouth, head swaying viciously from side to side, wicked eyes shining in the bright light from the chandelier. I saw the muscles in the creature's fore-part swell, and in a sort of horror-trance I watched its head dart forward, but, miraculously, it stopped its stroke halfway, and drew its head back, turning to glance menacingly at me first from one eye, then the other. Somehow, it seemed to me, the thing was playing with me as a cat might play a mouse, threatening, intimidating, letting me know it was master of the situation and could kill me any time it wished, but deliberately refraining from the death-stroke.

"With one leap I was in the middle of my bed, and when a squad of bellboys came running in response to the frantic call for help I telephoned, they found me crouched against the headboard, almost wild with fear.

"They turned the room completely inside out, rolling back the rugs, probing into chairs and sofa, emptying the bureau drawers, even taking down the towels from the bathroom rack, but nowhere was there any sign of the water moccasin that had terrified me. At the end of fifteen minutes' search they accepted half a dollar each and went grinning from the room. I knew it would be useless to appeal for help again, for I heard one whisper to another as they paused outside my door: 'It ain't right to let them Yankees loose in N'Orleans; they don't know how to hold their licker.'

I didn't take a train next morning. Somehow, I'd an idea — crazy as it seemed — that my promise to myself and the sudden, inexplicable appearance of the snake beside my foot were related in some way. Just after luncheon I thought I'd put the theory to a test.

"'Well,' I said aloud, 'I guess I might as well start packing. Don't want to let the sun go down and find me here —'

"My theory was right. I hadn't finished speaking when I heard the warning hiss, and there, poised ready for the stroke, the snake was coiled before the door. And it was no phantom, either, no figment of an overwrought imagination. It lay upon a rug the hotel management had placed before the door to take the wear of constant passage from the carpet, and I could see the high pile of the rug crushed down beneath its weight. It was flesh and scales — and fangs! — and it coiled and threatened me in my twelfth-floor room in the bright sunlight of the afternoon.

"Little chills of terror chased each other up my back, and I could feel the short hairs on my neck grow stiff and scratch against my collar, but I kept myself in hand. Pretending to ignore the loathsome thing, I flung myself upon the bed.

"'Oh, well,' I said aloud, 'there really isn't any need of hurrying. I promised Julie that I'd come to her tonight, and I mustn't disappoint her.'" Half a minute later I roused myself upon my elbow and glanced toward the door. The snake was gone.

"'Here's a letter for you, Mr. Minton,' said the desk clerk as I paused to leave my key. The note was on grey paper edged with silver-gilt, and very highly scented. The penmanship was tiny, stilted and ill-formed, as though the author were unused to writing, but I could make it out:

Adoré
  Meet me in St. Denis Cemetery at sunset À vous de coeur pour l'éternité
                                                                    JULIE

"I stuffed the note back in my pocket. The more I thought about the whole affair the less I liked it. The flirtation had begun harmlessly enough, and Julie was as lovely and appealing as a figure in a fairy-tale, but there are unpleasant aspects to most fairy-tales, and this was no exception. That scene last night when she had seemed to argue with a full-grown cottonmouth, and the mysterious appearance of the snake whenever I spoke of breaking my promise to go back to her — there was something too much like black magic in it. Now she addressed me as her adored and signed herself for eternity; finally named a graveyard as our rendezvous. Things had become a little bit too thick.

"I was standing at the corner of Canal and Baronne Streets, and crowds of office workers and late shoppers elbowed past me. 'I'll be damned if I'll meet her in a cemetery, or anywhere else,' I muttered. 'I've had enough of all this nonsense —'

"A woman's shrill scream, echoed by a man's hoarse shout of terror, interrupted me. On the marble pavement of Canal Street, with half a thousand people bustling by, lay coiled a three-foot water moccasin. Here was proof. I'd seen it twice in my room at the hotel, but I'd been alone each time. Some form of weird hypnosis might have made me think I saw it, but the screaming woman and the shouting man, these panic-stricken people in Canal Street, couldn't all be victims of a spell which had been cast on me. 'All right, I'll go,' I almost shouted, and instantly, as though it been but a puff of smoke, the snake was gone, the half-fainting woman and a crowd of curious bystanders asking what was wrong left to prove I had not been the victim of some strange delusion.

"Old Saint Denis Cemetery lay drowsing in the blue, faint twilight. It has no graves as we know them, for when the city was laid out it was below sea level and bodies were stored away in crypts set row on row like lines of pigeon-holes in walls as thick as those of mediæval castles. Grass-grown aisles run between the rows of vaults, and the effect is a true city of the dead with narrow streets shut in by close-set houses. The rattle of a trolley car in Rampart Street came to me faintly as I walked between the rows of tombs; from the river came the mellow-throated bellow of a steamer's whistle, but both sounds were muted as though heard from a great distance. The tomb-lined bastions of Saint Denis hold the present out as firmly as they hold the memories of the past within.

"Down one aisle and up another I walked, the close-clipped turf deadening my footfalls so I might have been a ghost come back to haunt the ancient burial ground, but nowhere was there sign or trace of Julie. I made the circuit of the labyrinth and finally paused before one of the more pretentious tombs.

"'Looks as if she'd stood me up,' I murmured. 'If she has, I have a good excuse to —'

"'But *non, mon coeur*, I have not disappointed you!' a soft voice whispered in my ear. 'See, I am here.'

"I think I must have jumped at sound of her greeting, for she clapped her hands delightedly before she put them on my shoulders and turned her face up for a kiss. 'Silly one,' she chided, 'did you think your Julie was unfaithful?'

"I put her hands away as gently as I could, for her utter self-surrender was embarrassing. 'Where were you?' I asked, striving to make neutral conversation. 'I've been prowling round this graveyard for the last half-hour, and came through this aisle not a minute ago, but I didn't see you —'

"'Ah, but I saw you, *chéri*; I have watched you as you made your solemn rounds like a watchman of the night. *Ohé*, but it was hard to wait until the sun went down to greet you, *mon petit!*'

"She laughed again, and her mirth was mellowly musical as the gurgle of cool water poured from a silver vase.

"'How could you have seen me?' I demanded. 'Where were you all this time?'

"But here, of course,' she answered naïvely, resting one hand against the greystone slab that sealed the tomb.

"I shook my head bewilderedly. The tomb, like all the others in the deeply recessed wall, was of rough cement incrusted with small seashells, and its sides were straight and blank without a spear of ivy clinging to them. A sparrow could not have found cover there, yet. . . .

"Julie raised herself on tiptoe and stretched her arms out right and left while she looked at me through half-closed, smiling eyes. *Je suis engourdie* — I am stiff with sleep,' she told me, stifling a yawn. 'But now that you are come, *mon cher*, I am wakeful as the pussy-cat that rouses at the scampering of the mouse. Come, let us walk in this garden of mine.' She linked her arm through mine and started down the grassy, grave-lined path.

"Tiny shivers — not of cold — were flickering through my cheeks and down my neck beneath my ears. I *had* to have an explanation . . . the snake, her declaration that she watched me as I searched the cemetery — and from a tomb where a beetle could not have found a hiding place — her announcement she was still stiff from sleeping, now her reference to a half-forgotten graveyard as her garden.

"'See here, I want to know —' I started, but she laid her hand across my lips.

"'Do not ask to know too soon, *mon coeur,*' she bade. 'Look at me, am I not veritably *élégante?*' She stood back a step, gathered up her skirts and swept me a deep curtsy.

"There was no denying she was beautiful. Her tightly curling hair had been combed high and tied back with a fillet of bright violet tissue which bound her brows like a diadem and at the front of which an aigret plume was set. In her ears were hung two beautifully matched cameos, outlined in gold and seed-pearls, and almost large as silver dollars; a necklace of antique dull-gold hung round her throat, and its pendant was a duplicate of her ear-cameos, while a bracelet of matt-gold set with a fourth matched anaglyph was clasped about her left arm just above the elbow. Her gown was sheer white muslin, low cut at front and back, with little puff-sleeves at the shoulders, fitted tightly at the bodice and flaring sharply from a high-set waist. Over it she wore a narrow scarf of violet silk, hung behind her neck and dropping down on either side in front like a clergy-man's stole. Her sandals were gilt leather, heel-less as a ballet dancer's shoes and laced with violet ribbons. Her lovely, pearl-white hands were bare of rings, but on the second toe of her right foot there showed a little cameo which matched the others which she wore.

"I could feel my heart begin to pound and my breath come quicker as I looked at her, but:

"'You look as if you're going to a masquerade,' I said.

"A look of hurt surprize showed in her eyes. 'A masquerade?' she echoed. 'But no, it is my best, my very finest, that I wear for you tonight, *mon adoré*. Do not you like it; do you not love me, Édouard?'

"'No,' I answered shortly, 'I do not. We might as well understand each other, Julie. I'm not in love with you and I never was. It's been a pretty flirtation, nothing more. I'm going home tomorrow, and —'

"'But you will come again? Surely you will come again?' she pleaded, 'You cannot mean it when you say you do not love me, Édouard. Tell me that you spoke so but to tease me —'

"A warning hiss sounded in the grass beside my foot, but I was too angry to be frightened. 'Go ahead, set your devilish snake on me,' I taunted. 'Let it bite me. I'd as soon be dead as —'

"The snake was quick, but Julie quicker. In the split-second required for the thing to drive at me she leaped across the grass-grown aisle and pushed me back. So violent was the shove she gave me that I fell against the tomb, struck my head against a small projecting stone and stumbled to my knees. As I fought for footing on the slippery grass I saw the deadly, wedge-shaped head strike full against the girl's bare ankle and heard her gasp with pain. The snake recoiled and swung its head toward me, but Julie dropped down to her knees and spread her arms protectingly about me.

"'*Non, non, grand'tante!*' she screamed; 'not this one! Let me —' Her voice broke on a little gasp and with a retching hiccup she sank limply to the grass.

"I tried to rise, but my foot slipped on the grass and I fell back heavily against the tomb, crashing my brow against its shell-set cement wall. I saw Julie lying in a little huddled heap of white against the blackness of the sward, and, shadowy but clearly visible, an aged, wrinkled Negress with turbaned head and cambric apron bending over her, nursing her head against her bosom and rocking back and forth grotesquely while she crooned a wordless threnody. Where had she come from? I wondered idly. Where had the snake gone? Why did the moonlight seem to fade and flicker like a dying lamp? Once more I tried to rise, but slipped back to the grass before the tomb as everything went black before me.

"The lavender light of early morning was streaming over the tomb-walls of the cemetery when I waked. I lay quiet for a little while, wondering sleepily how I came there. Then, just as the first rays of the sun shot through the thinning shadows, I remembered. Julie! The snake had bitten her when she flung herself before me. She was gone; the old Negress — where had *she* come from? — was gone, too, and I was utterly alone in the old graveyard.

"Stiff from lying on the ground, I got myself up awkwardly, grasping at the flower-shelf projecting from the tomb. As my eyes came level with the slab that sealed the crypt I felt the breath catch in my throat. The crypt, like all its fellows, looked for all the world like an old oven let into a brick wall overlaid with peeling plaster. The sealing-stone was probably once white, but years had stained it to a dirty grey, and time had all but rubbed its legend out. Still, I could see the faint inscription carved in quaint, old-fashioned letters, and disbelief gave way to incredulity, which was replaced by panic terror as I read:

Ici repose malheureusement
Julie Amelie Marie d'Ayen
Nationale de Paris France
Née le 29 Aout 1788
Décédée a la N O le 2 Juillet 1807

"Julie! Little Julie whom I'd held in my arms, whose mouth had lain on mine in eager kisses, was a corpse! Dead and in her grave more than a century!"

*T*he silence lengthened. Ned stared miserably before him, his outward eyes unseeing, but his mind's eye turned upon that scene in old Saint Denis Cemetery. De Grandin tugged and tugged again at the ends of his mustache till I thought he'd drag the hairs out by the roots. I could think of nothing which might ease the tension till:

"Of course, the name cut on the tombstone was a piece of pure coincidence," I hazarded. "Most likely the young woman deliberately assumed it to mislead you —"

"And the snake which threatened our young friend, he was an assumption, also, one infers?" de Grandin interrupted.

"N-o, but it could have been a trick. Ned saw an aged Negress in the cemetery, and those old Southern darkies have strange powers —"

"I damn think that you hit the thumb upon the nail that time, my friend," the little Frenchman nodded, "though you do not realize how accurate your diagnosis is." To Ned:

"Have you seen this snake again since coming North?"

"Yes," Ned replied. "I have. I was too stunned to speak when I read the epitaph, and I wandered back to the hotel in a sort of daze and packed my bags in silence. Possibly that's why there was no further visitation there. I don't know. I do know nothing further happened, though, and when several months had passed with nothing but my memories to remind me of the incident, I began to think I'd suffered from some sort of walking nightmare. Nella and I went ahead with preparations for our wedding, but three weeks ago the postman brought me this —"

He reached into an inner pocket and drew out an envelope. It was of soft grey paper, edged with silver-gilt, and the address was in tiny, almost unreadable script:

M. Édouard Minton,
    30 Rue Carteret 30,
        Harrisonville, N. J.

"U'm?" de Grandin commented as he inspected it. "It is addressed à la française. And the letter, may one read it?"

"Of course," Ned answered. "I'd like you to."

Across de Grandin's shoulder I made out the hast-ily-scrawled missive:

Adoré
Remember your promise and the kiss of blood that
sealed it. Soon I shall call and you must come.
Pour le temps et pour l'éternité,

JULIE

"You recognize the writing?" de Grandin asked. "It is —"

"Oh, yes," Ned answered bitterly, "I recognize it; it's the same the other note was written in."

"And then?"

The boy smiled bleakly. "I crushed the thing into a ball and threw it on the floor and stamped on it. Swore I'd die before I'd keep another rendezvous with her, and —" He broke off, and put trembling hands up to his face.

"The so mysterious serpent came again, one may assume?" de Grandin prompted.

"But it's only a phantom snake," I interjected. "At worst it's nothing more than a terrifying vision —"

"Think so?" Ned broke in. "D'ye remember Rowdy, my airedale terrier?"

I nodded.

"He was in the room when I opened this letter, and when the cottonmouth appeared beside me on the floor he made a dash for it. Whether it would have struck me I don't know, but it struck at him as he leaped and caught him squarely in the throat. He thrashed and fought, and the thing held on with locked jaws till I grabbed a fire-shovel and made for it; then, before I could strike, it vanished.

"But its venom didn't. Poor old Rowdy was dead before I could get him out of the house, but I took his corpse to Doctor Kirchoff, the veterinary, and told him Rowdy died suddenly and I wanted him to make an autopsy. He went back to his operating-room and stayed there half an hour. When he came back to the office he was wiping his glasses and wore the most astonished look I've ever seen on a human face. 'You say your dog died suddenly — in the house?' he asked.

"'Yes,' I told him; 'just rolled over and died.'

"'Well, bless my soul, that's the most amazing thing I ever heard!' he answered. 'I can't account for it. That dog died from snake-bite; copperhead, I'd say, and the marks of the fangs show plainly on his throat.'"

"But I thought you said it was a water moccasin," I objected. "Now Doctor Kirchoff says it was a copper-head —"

"*Ah hah!*" de Grandin laughed a thought unpleasantly. "Did no one ever tell you that the copperhead and moccasin are of close kind, my friend? Have not you heard some ophiologists maintain the moccasin is but a dark variety of copperhead?" He did not pause for my reply, but turned again to Ned:

"One understands your chivalry, *Monsieur.* For yourself you have no fear, since after all at times life can be bought too dearly, but the death of your small dog has put a different aspect on the matter. If this never-to-be-sufficiently-anathematized serpent which comes and goes like the *boîte à surprise* — the how do you call him? Jack from the box? — is enough a ghost thing to appear at any time and place it wills, but sufficiently physical to exude venom which will kill a strong and healthy terrier, you have the fear for Mademoiselle Nella, *n'est-ce-pas?*"

"Precisely, you —"

"And you are well advised to have the caution, my young friend. We face a serious condition."

"What do you advise?"

The Frenchman teased his needlepoint mustache-tip with a thoughtful thumb and forefinger. "For the present, nothing," he replied at length. "Let me look this situation over; let me view it from all angles. Whatever I might tell you now would probably be wrong. Suppose we meet again one week from now. By that time I should have my data well in hand."

"And in the meantime —"

"Continue to be coy with Mademoiselle Nella. Perhaps it would be well if you recalled important business which requires that you leave town till you hear from me again. There is no need to put her life in peril at this time."

"*I*f it weren't for Kirchoff's testimony I'd say Ned Minton had gone raving crazy," I declared as the door closed on our visitors. "The whole thing's wilder than an opium smoker's dream — that meeting with the girl in New Orleans, the snake that comes and disappears, the assignation in the cemetery — it's all too preposterous. But I know Kirchoff. He's as unimaginative as a side of sole-leather, and as efficient as he is unimaginative. If he says Minton's dog died of snake-bite that's what it died of, but the whole affair's so utterly fantastic —"

"Agreed," de Grandin nodded; "but what is fantasy but the appearance of mental images as such, severed from ordinary relations? The 'ordinary relations' of images are those to which we are accustomed, which conform to our experience. The wider that experience, the more ordinary will we find extraordinary relations. By example, take yourself: You sit in a dark auditorium and see a railway train come rushing at you. Now, it is not at all in ordinary experience for a locomotive to come dashing in a theater filled with people, it is quite otherwise; but you keep your seat, you do not flinch, you are not frightened. It is nothing but a motion picture, which you understand. But if you were a savage from New Guinea you would rise and fly in panic from this steaming, shrieking iron monster which bears down on you. *Tiens,* it is a matter of experience, you see. To you it is an everyday event, to the savage it would be a new and terrifying thing.

"Or, perhaps, you are at the hospital. You place a patient between you and the Crookes' tube of an X-ray, you turn on the current, you observe him through the fluoroscope and *pouf!* his flesh all melts away and his bones spring out in sharp relief. Three hundred years ago you would have howled like a stoned dog at the sight, and prayed to be delivered from the witchcraft which produced it. Today you curse and swear like twenty drunken pirates if the Röntgenologist is but thirty seconds late in setting up the apparatus. These things are 'scientific,' you understand their underlying formulæ, therefore they seem natural. But mention what you please to call the occult, and you scoff, and that is but admitting that you are opposed to something which you do not understand. The credible and believable is that to which we are accustomed, the fantastic and incredible is what we cannot explain in terms of previous experience. *Voilà, c'est très simple, n'est-ce-pas?*"

"You mean to say you understand all this?"

"Not at all by any means; I am clever, me, but not that clever. No, my friend, I am as much in the dark as you, only I do not refuse to credit what our young friend tells us. I believe the things he has related happened, exactly as he has recounted them. I do not understand, but I believe. Accordingly, I must probe, I must sift, I must examine this matter. We see it now as a group of unrelated and irrelevant occurrences, but somewhere lies the key which will enable us to make harmony from this discord, to gather these stray, tangled threads into an ordered pattern. I go to seek that key."

"Where?"

"To New Orleans, of course. Tonight I pack my portmanteaux, tomorrow I entrain. Just now" — he smothered a tremendous yawn — "now I do what every wise man does as often as he can. I take a drink."

*S*even evenings later we gathered in my study, de Grandin, Ned and I, and from the little Frenchman's shining eyes I knew his quest had been productive of results.

"My friends," he told us solemnly, "I am a clever person, and a lucky one, as well. The morning after my arrival at New Orleans I enjoyed three Ramos fizzes, then went to sit in City Park by the old Dueling-Oak and wished with all my heart that I had taken four. And while I sat in self-reproachful thought, sorrowing for the drink that I had missed, behold, one passed by whom I recognized. He was my old schoolfellow, Paul Dubois, now a priest in holy orders and attached to the Cathedral of Saint Louis.

"He took me to his quarters, that good, pious man, and gave me luncheon. It was Friday and a fast day, so we fasted. *Mon Dieu,* but we did fast! On créole gumbo and oysters à la Rockefeller, and baked pompano and little shrimp fried crisp in olive oil and chicory salad and seven different kinds of cheese and wine. When we were so filled with fasting that we could not eat another morsel my old friend took me to another priest, a native of New Orleans whose stock of local lore was second only to his marvelous capacity for fine champagne. *Morbleu,* how I admire that one! And now, attend me very carefully, my friends. What he disclosed to me makes many hidden mysteries all clear:

"In New Orleans there lived a wealthy family named d'Ayen. They possessed much gold and land, a thousand slaves or more, and one fair daughter by the name of Julie. When this country bought the Louisiana Territory from Napoléon and your army came to occupy the forts, this young girl fell in love with a young officer, a Lieutenant Philip Merriwell. *Tenez,* army love in those times was no different than it is today, it seems. This gay young lieutenant, he came, he wooed, he won, he rode away, and little Julie wept and sighed and finally died of heartbreak. In her lovesick illness she had for constant company a slave, an old mulatress known to most as Maman Dragonne, but to Julie simply as *grand'tante,* great-aunt. She had nursed our little Julie at the breast, and all her life she fostered and attended her. To her little white *'mamselle'* she was all gentleness and kindness, but to others she was fierce and frightful, for she was a 'conjon woman,' adept at obeah, the black magic of the Congo, and among the blacks she ruled as queen by force of fear, while the whites were wont to treat her with respect and, it was more than merely whispered, retain her services upon occasion. She could sell protection to the duelist, and he who bore her charm would surely conquer on the field of honor; she brewed love-drafts which turned the hearts and heads of the most capricious coquettes or the most constant wives, as occasion warranted; by merely staring fixedly at someone she could cause him to take sick and die, and — here we commence to tread upon our own terrain — she was said to have the power of changing to a snake at will.

"Very good. You follow? When poor young Julie died of heartbreak it was old Maman Dragonne — the little white one's *grand'tante* — who watched beside her bed. It is said she stood beside her mistress' coffin and called a curse upon the fickle lover; swore he would come back and die beside the body of the sweetheart he deserted. She also made a prophecy. Julie should have many loves, but her body should not know corruption nor her spirit rest until she could find one to keep his promise and return to her with words of love upon his lips. Those who failed her should die horribly, but he who kept his pledge would bring her rest and peace. This augury she made while she stood beside her mistress' coffin just before they sealed it in the tomb in old Saint Denis Cemetery. Then she disappeared."

"You mean she ran away?" I asked.

"I mean she disappeared, vanished, evanesced, evaporated. She was never seen again, not even by the people who stood next to her when she pronounced her prophecy."

"But —"

"No buts, my friend, if you will be so kind. Years later, when the British stormed New Orleans, Lieutenant Merriwell was there with General Andrew Jackson. He survived the battle like a man whose life is charmed, though all around him comrades fell and three horses were shot under him. Then, when the strife was done, he went to the grand banquet tendered to the victors. While gayety was at its height he abruptly left the table. Next morning he was found upon the grass before the tomb of Julie d'Ayen. He was dead. He died from snake-bite.

"The years marched on and stories spread about the town, stories of a strange and lovely *belle dame sans merci,* a modern Circe who lured young gallants to their doom. Time and again some gay young blade of New Orleans would boast a conquest. Passing late at night through Royal Street, he would have a flower dropped to him as he walked underneath a balcony. He would meet a lovely girl dressed in the early Empire style, and be surprized at the ease with which he pushed his suit; then — upon the trees in Chartres Street appeared his funeral notices. He was dead, invariably he was dead of snake-bite. *Parbleu,* it got to be a saying that he who died mysteriously must have met the Lady of the Moonlight as he walked through Royal Street!"

He paused and poured a thimbleful of brandy in his coffee. "You see?" he asked.

"No, I'm shot if I do!" I answered. "I can't see the connection between —"

"Night and breaking dawn, perhaps?" he asked sarcastically. "If two and two make four, my friend, and even you will not deny they do, then these things I have told you give an explanation of our young friend's trouble. This girl he met was most indubitably Julie, poor little Julie d'Ayen on whose tombstone it is carved: '*Ici repose malheureusement* — here lies unhappily.' The so mysterious snake which menaces young Monsieur Minton is none other than the aged Maman Dragonne — *grand'tante,* as Julie called her."

"But Ned's already failed to keep his tryst," I objected. "Why didn't this snake-woman sting him in the hotel, or —"

"Do you recall what Julie said when first the snake appeared?" he interrupted. "'Not this one, *grand'tante!*' And again, in the old cemetery when the serpent actually struck at him, she threw herself before him and received the blow. It could not permanently injure her;

to earthly injuries the dead are proof, but the shock of it caused her to swoon, it seems. *Monsieur,"* he bowed to Ned, "you are more fortunate than any of those others. Several times you have been close to death, but each time you escaped. You have been given chance and chance again to keep your pledged word to the dead, a thing no other faithless lover of the little Julie ever had. It seems, Monsieur, this dead girl truly loves you."

"How horrible!" I muttered.

"You said it, Doctor Trowbridge!" Ned seconded. "It looks as if I'm in a spot, all right."

"Mais non," de Grandin contradicted. "Escape is obvious, my friend."

"How, in heaven's name?"

"Keep your promised word; go back to her."

"Good Lord, I can't do that! Go back to a corpse, take her in my arms — kiss her?"

"Certainement, why not?"

"Why — why, she's *dead!"*

"Is she not beautiful?"

"She's lovely and alluring as a siren's song. I think she's the most exquisite thing I've ever seen, but —" he rose and walked unsteadily across the room. "If it weren't for Nella," he said slowly, "I might not find it hard to follow your advice. Julie's sweet and beautiful, and artless and affectionate as a child; kind, too, the way she stood between me and that awful snake-thing, but — oh, it's out of the question!"

"Then we must expand the question to accommodate it, my friend. For the safety of the living — for Mademoiselle Nella's sake — and for the repose of the dead, you must keep the oath you swore to little Julie d'Ayen. You must go back to New Orleans and keep your rendezvous."

*T*he dead of old Saint Denis lay in dreamless sleep beneath the palely argent rays of the fast-waxing moon. The ovenlike tombs were gay with hardly-wilted flowers; for two days before was All Saints' Day, and no grave in all New Orleans is so lowly, no dead so long interred, that pious hands do not bear blossoms of remembrance to them on that feast of memories.

De Grandin had been busily engaged all afternoon, making mysterious trips to the old Negro quarter in company with a patriarchal scion of Indian and Negro ancestry who professed ability to guide him to the city's foremost practitioner of voodoo; returning to the hotel only to dash out again to consult his friend at the Cathedral; coming back to stare with thoughtful eyes upon the changing panorama of Canal Street while Ned, nervous as a race-horse at the barrier, tramped up and down the room lighting cigarette from cigarette and drinking absinthe frappés alternating with sharp, bitter sazarac cocktails till I wondered that he did not fall in utter alcoholic collapse. By evening I had that eery feeling that the sane experience when alone with mad folk. I was ready to shriek at any unexpected noise or turn and run at sight of a strange shadow.

"My friend," de Grandin ordered as we reached the grass-paved corridor of tombs where Ned had told us the d'Ayen vaults were, "I suggest that you drink this." From an inner pocket he drew out a tiny flask of ruby glass and snapped its stopper loose. A strong and slightly acrid scent came to me, sweet and spicy, faintly reminiscent of the odor of the aromatic herbs one smells about a mummy's wrappings.

"Thanks, I've had enough to drink already," Ned said shortly.

"You are informing me, *mon vieux?*" the little Frenchman answered with a smile. "It is for that I brought this draft along. It will help you draw yourself together. You have need of all your faculties this time, believe me."

Ned put the bottle to his lips, drained its contents, hiccuped lightly, then braced his shoulders. "That *is* a pick-up," he complimented. "Too bad you didn't let me have it sooner, sir. I think I can go through the ordeal now."

"One is sure you can," the Frenchman answered confidently. "Walk slowly toward the spot where you last saw Julie, if you please. We shall await you here, in easy call if we are needed."

The aisle of tombs was empty as Ned left us. The turf had been fresh-mown for the day of visitation and was as smooth and short as a lawn tennis court. A field-mouse could not have run across the pathway without our seeing it. This much I noticed idly as Ned trudged away from us, walking more like a man on his way to the gallows than one who went to keep a lovers' rendezvous . . . and suddenly he was not alone. There was another with him, a girl dressed in a clinging robe of sheer white muslin cut in the charming fashion of the First Empire, girdled high beneath the bosom with a sash of light-blue ribbon. A wreath of pale gardenias lay upon her bright, fair hair; her slender arms were pearl-white in the moonlight. As she stepped toward Ned I thought involuntarily of a line from Sir John Suckling:

"Her feet . . . like little mice stole in and out."

"*Édouard, chêri! O, coeur de mon coeur, c'est véritablement toi?* Thou hast come willingly, unasked, *petit amant?*"

"I'm here," Ned answered steadily, "but only —" He paused and drew a sudden gasping breath, as though a hand had been laid on his throat.

"*Chèri,*" the girl asked in a trembling voice, "you are cold to me; do not you love me, then — you are not here because your heart heard my heart calling? O heart of my heart's heart, if you but knew how I have longed and waited! It has been *triste, mon Édouard,* lying in my narrow bed alone while winter rains and summer suns beat down, listening for your footfall. I could have gone out at my pleasure whenever moonlight made the nights all bright with silver; I could have sought for other lovers, but I would not. You held release for me within your hands, and if I might not have it from you I would forfeit it forever. Do not you bring release for me, my Édouard? Say that it is so!"

An odd look came into the boy's face. He might have seen her for the first time, and been dazzled by her beauty and the winsome sweetness of her voice.

"Julie!" he whispered softly. "Poor, patient, faithful little Julie!"

In a single stride he crossed the intervening turf and was on his knees before her, kissing her hands, the hem of her gown, her sandaled feet, and babbling half-coherent, broken words of love.

She put her hands upon his head as if in benediction, then turned them, holding them palm-forward to his lips, finally crooked her fingers underneath his chin and raised his face. "Nay, love, sweet love, art thou a worshipper and I a saint that thou should kneel to me?" she asked him tenderly. "See, my lips are famishing for thine, and wilt thou waste thy kisses on my hands and feet and garment? Make haste, my heart, we have but little time, and I would know the kisses of redemption ere —"

They clung together in the moonlight, her white-robed, lissome form and his somberly-clad body seemed to melt and merge in one while her hands reached up to clasp his cheeks and draw his face down to her yearning, scarlet mouth.

De Grandin was reciting something in a mumbling monotone; his words were scarcely audible, but I caught a phrase occasionally: "... rest eternal grant to her, O Lord ... let light eternal shine upon her ... from the gates of hell her soul deliver. ... *Kyrie eleison.* ..."

"Julie!" we heard Ned's despairing cry, and:

"*Ha*, it comes, it has begun; it finishes!" de Grandin whispered gratingly.

The girl had sunk down to the grass as though she swooned; one arm had fallen limply from Ned's shoulder, but the other still was clasped about his neck as we raced toward them. "*Adieu, mon amoureux; adieu pour ce monde, adieu pour l'autre; adieu pour l'éternité!*" we heard her sob. When we reached him, Ned knelt empty-armed before the tomb. Of Julie there was neither sign nor trace.

"So, assist him, if you will, my friend," de Grandin bade, motioning me to take Ned's elbow. "Help him to the gate. I follow quickly, but first I have a task to do."

As I led Ned, staggering like a drunken man, toward the cemetery exit, I heard the clang of metal striking metal at the tomb behind us.

"*W*hat did you stop behind to do?" I asked as we prepared for bed at the hotel.

He flashed his quick, infectious smile at me, and tweaked his mustache ends, for all the world like a self-satisfied tomcat furbishing his whiskers after finishing a bowl of cream. "There was an alteration to that epitaph I had to make. You recall it read, '*Ici repose malheureusement* — here lies unhappily Julie d'Ayen'? That is no longer true. I chiseled off the *malheureuse-ment*. Thanks to Monsieur Édouard's courage and my cleverness the old one's prophecy was fulfilled tonight; and poor, small Julie has found rest at last. Tomorrow morning they celebrate the first of a series of masses I have arranged for her at the Cathedral."

"What was that drink you gave Ned just before he left us?" I asked curiously. "It smelled like —"

"*Le bon Dieu* and the devil know — not I," he answered with a grin. "It was a voodoo love-potion. I found the realization that she had been dead a century and more so greatly troubled our young friend that he swore he could not be affectionate to our poor Julie; so I went down to the Negro quarter in the afternoon and arranged to have a philtre brewed. *Eh bien,* that aged black one who concocted it assured me that she could inspire love for the image of a crocodile in the heart of anyone who looked upon it after taking but a drop of her decoction, and she charged me twenty dollars for it. But I think I had my money's worth. Did it not work marvelously?"

"Then Julie's really gone? Ned's coming back released her from the spell —"

"Not wholly gone," he corrected. "Her little body now is but a small handful of dust, her spirit is no longer earth-bound, and the familiar demon who in life was old Maman Dragonne has left the earth with her, as well. No longer will she metamorphosize into a snake and kill the faithless ones who kiss her little mistress and then forswear their troth, but — *non,* my friend, Julie is not gone entirely, I think. In the years to come when Ned and Nella have long been joined in wedded bliss, there will be minutes when Julie's face and Julie's voice and the touch of Julie's little hands will haunt his memory. There will always be one little corner of his heart which never will belong to Madame Nella Minton, for it will be forever Julie's. Yes, I think that it is so."

Slowly, deliberately, almost ritualistically, he poured a glass of wine and raised it. "To you, my little poor one," he said softly as he looked across the sleeping city toward old Saint Denis Cemetery. "You quit earth with a kiss upon your lips; may you sleep serene in Paradise until another kiss shall waken you."